by
Eloise Greenfield
Illustrated by
John Steptoe

HarperTrophy
A Division of HarperCollins*Publishers*

Library of Congress Cataloging-in-Publication Data
Greenfield, Eloise.
    She come bringing me that little baby girl.
    Summary: A child's disappointment and jealousy over a new baby sister
are dispelled as he becomes aware of the importance of his new role as a
big brother.
    [1. Brothers and sisters—Fiction]   I. Steptoe, John, date, illus.
II. Title.   PZ7.G845Sh   [E]   74-8104   ISBN 0-397-31586-4

A Scott Foresman Edition
ISBN 0-673-80122-5

For Steve and Monica
and all other Black brothers and sisters
who love and take care of each other

I asked Mama to bring me a little brother from the hospital, but she come bringing me that little baby girl wrapped all up in a pink blanket. Me and Aunt Mildred were looking out the window when Daddy brought them home.

I was glad to see Mama even if she didn't bring me what I wanted. When she got out of the car, I ran to the door to meet her.

Mama hugged me hard. She was glad to see me, too.
But she only had one arm to hug me with 'cause she
didn't put that little girl down for a minute.

Daddy helped them upstairs to the bedroom, but he didn't forget me. He said, "Come on, Kevin. We got to see what this baby's all about."

Mama sat on the bed and Aunt Mildred unwrapped the baby real slow and careful. It was a girl, all right, 'cause her fingers were way too small. She'd never be able to throw my football to me.

I didn't like her anyway. She cried too loud.

Not only that, she didn't look new with all those wrinkles in her face.

And not only that, I didn't like the way Mama and Daddy looked at her. Like she was the only baby in the world.

Then Aunt Barbara came with a big box tied in a long shiny ribbon. For the baby. She said, "Hi, Kevin." But she was looking at that little girl when she said it.

And Uncle Roy came with another box. He slapped me on my head and said, "How you doing, man?" But he didn't pick me up and swing me around like he always does.

Mrs. Moore from across the street came, and she had a present, too. She didn't even see me. All she said was, "Where's the baby? Where's the baby?"

It was making me sick to see them crowding around that ugly old baby and making those stupid noises. And presents all over the place. It was really making me sick.

So I put my chair by the window and just sat there, looking out at a squirrel running across the wire. I wasn't thinking about that old squirrel, though. I sure wasn't.

The next thing I know, Mama come bringing me that little baby girl and putting her right in my lap. I didn't even look down at that baby.

Daddy brought Mama a chair and she sat down beside me. She helped me hold the baby with one of her arms and she put her other arm around me.

"You're a big brother now," Mama said.

"I don't want to be a brother to no girl," I said.

"But I need you to help me take care of her," Mama said.

I said, "You do?"

Mama smiled at me and hugged me tight with that one arm. "Yes, I do," she said. "And you know what?"

I said, "What?"

"I used to be a baby girl," she said.

I said, "You did?" I looked up at Mama and down at that baby.

"Uh-huh," Mama said. "And my big brother used to help take care of me."

"I sure did," Uncle Roy said. "I wouldn't let nobody bother my little sister."

I tried to think of how they looked. Mama as a baby and Uncle Roy as a boy. It was so funny, I laughed right out loud.

I couldn't laugh too hard, though. I didn't want to break the baby.

I looked at her again and she wasn't all that ugly anymore. She was a little bit cute, even with the wrinkles.

I gave the baby back to Mama. "I got to go get Kenny and show him my sister," I said.

"Hurry back, man," Uncle Roy said. "You still got that swing coming."

I got Kenny, and Debra too. And they just stood
there looking at my sister like they had never seen a
baby that pretty before.

I was watching them, though. I had to be sure they didn't squeeze her too hard or anything.

You know, when my sister's fingers grow some, maybe I can show her how to throw a football. If she uses both hands.

And she can have one of Mama's arms, too. As long as she knows the other one is mine.